COFFEE IN THE WOODS

By Lotus R Flower & Empress Simone

This novel is a work of Fiction. Any resemblances to actual events, real people, living or dead, organizations, locales, or establishments are products of the Author's imagination. Other names, characters, places, and incidents are used fictitiously.

Chapter 1
Click Clack

Coffee raced for the elevator. But, unfortunately, she was late yet again. The new executive that contracted her services was a stickler for promptness, but that just wasn't in Coffee's nature.

Her Manolo's were working double time. One would have thought she was Jackie Joyner Kersee in her prime.

Click-clack, click-clack was all you heard as Coffee raced toward the sea of white faces staring at her but not caring enough to hold open the elevator doors.

"Damn, " she uttered, making it inside before the doors slammed shut. Then she noticed John smirking at her. He was an asshole in every sense of the word. She couldn't put her finger on it, but something was off about him.

Shaking off the jitters, she straightened out her black pencil skirt. Coffee could still feel his eyes on her. She looked at him as if to say, ”May I help you?” but caught herself before her mouth started to talk.

The elevator couldn't move fast enough. She didn't have time for childish games. The meeting with Bryson and Gordon Medical Firm was one of the most important of her career.

If all went well, not only would she bring in a six-figure deal for her corporation, but it would be a good look amongst her peers in the corporate world.

It would also prove Coffee had a niche for making her mark on a less diverse environment that was different from her ”*norm.*”

”Good morning, ” she greeted the staff in the brightly lit conference room.

”Good morning Ms. Hart. We were just ready to get started, ” O'Leary replied.

”Where should I set up?”

"The wall to your far right."

Coffee prepared her PowerPoint presentation, which she worked diligently on for the past three weeks.

O'Leary concluded the meeting after showing the staff why it would be wise to choose Coopers' Financial Services Unlimited (can be changed).

"Ms. Hart"

"Coffee. Please call me Coffee."

"Sure...Coffee, would you like to stay and have coffee with us?" he questioned with a slight giggle, amused with himself.

Coffee thought his joke was corny as hell, but she kept her poker face and obliged them in the offer. Being offered to stay back after the presentation was a great sign that the executives wanted to do business. As Coffee walked over in their direction, she could not help thinking to herself, “black girl magic.”

“I must confess I was utterly impressed by your presentation, Coffee,” O’Leary exclaimed. “What do you need to do to complete this project within three months”?

Coffee glared out of the large office window towards the skyline and mumbled, “a change in scenery.”

The city is very high paced and, quite honestly, can be very overwhelming with the hustle and bustle daily. Coffee has completed some of her best work being reclusive.

Although it was hard to turn the noise off, she did. Her career meant everything to her and getting out of the city was her main priority. She was determined to break the cycle within her family. A mundane job wasn’t her destiny. Coffee aspired to have and be more than what her environment had to offer.

"Coffee, what will it take?" O'Leary shouted in enthusiasm

"Let's see; I would like to be somewhere enjoying nature; I would like an advance to pay all my bills for three months and an assistance paid for by the corporation's budget, of course."

"Sure, not a problem at all, Coffee. Find the location, and I'll have my secretary Joseline take care of the rest."

And with a firm handshake just like that, the deal was set into motion.

Coffee was trying to maintain her poise and professionalism. O'Leary wanting to contract her services was the first time Coffee's requirements were met without resistance and haggling. She felt damned good and knew the promotion was not only within her sights but within her grasp. But first, Coffee was going to enjoy her time in the woods. Then, she'd be free to commune with mother nature.

Chapter 2

The whirl of the helicopter's propellers to take Coffee from the airport to the cabin Mr. O'Leary's assistant reserved for her was exhilarating. It did something to her. She felt such a serene feeling she didn't want the ride to end. Killington Peak was breathtaking. Who would have thought Vermont would be so beautiful?

When the helicopter touched down, and the pilot assisted her out of the copter, Coffee lost her breath once again. The area was so exquisite; it was something straight out of a magazine such as Home and Garden.

She imagined the upper echelon sipping hot cocoa by the fireplace with a bottle of Moet on ice nearby while the hostess served them warm pastries in the dining lodge.

Coffee was shocked and almost brought to tears when she noticed the hiking gear and guide holding a sign with her name "Coffee Hart!"

Coffee's tough-girl exterior was shed. She was free to be herself. The one everybody felt was weird. She wasn't odd, bougie, or eccentric; she was just not the norm.

Coffee enjoyed a good party every once in a while, but it wasn't a regular thing. So she'd instead wrap up under her blanket with a good book and a warm cup of tea spiked with a bit of liquor; nothing vital just enough for a good buzz.

Coffee liked poetry and spoken word nights. The ideal date for her was karaoke and not dinner and a movie. Her friends thought it was *white girl stuff,* but truth be told, she liked being *different.* Not quite the extrovert, not quite the introvert but a bit of both suited her just fine.

"I'm Coffee Hart."
"Nice to meet you. Please follow me," the guide replied.

He led her through a narrow path filled with beautiful snow-covered trees. Coffee now felt like the tourists who *oohed and ahhed* at the sights in Midtown Manhattan.

By the time they reached the cabin, Coffee was happy she wore her Timberlands and not her running shoes. The place was breathtaking. It held old oakwood country-style furniture. The bed looked larger than a California king bed, and the fireplace looked bigger than her bathroom at home. She raced to it and blew into her hands.

"I'll stoke the fire for you," the guide said.
"Thank you...I'm sorry, but what's your name?" she asked.
"Hylton.
"Well, thank you, Hylton, for being of great service."

Hylton discussed some much-needed information with Coffee about her three-month stay at the mountain hideaway. Since she had never been skiing, he instructed her regarding training times on the bunny slopes. He assured her that she would graduate from the novice level of skiing in the Bear Mountain region to the intermediate range within a week. After his reassurance and a bit more small talk, he left just as quickly as he arrived.

Coffee took a running leap and dived on the enormous bed. She stared around the room in sheer awe taking in the rustic decor. Not one for harming God's creatures, but she had to admit the white-tailed deer and the moose antlers hanging about were gorgeous and pristine.

Coffee unpacked her bags, placing her clothes neatly in the large five-drawer chest. She went into the bathroom; once again, she was in awe. It was dimly lit, but the fluffy, white towels and washcloths, trimmed with gold and embroidered with her initials, were just the appreciation she needed to be shown.

"Gee. Mr. O'Leary went all out for this event. I hope he doesn't want more than my business acumen," Coffee thought out loud, giggling slightly. She ran the hot water to the shower then grabbed the soap in the bamboo dish placed as a complimentary gift.

She took a sniff. It was all-natural and smelled like apple spice, her favorite. "*How'd he know?*" Coffee thought that was strange. Although they conversed about some of her likes, her favorite scents were not one of the topics.

After bathing and shampooing her jet-black short pixie cut hair, she dressed in her mountain gear and hit the bike trails. There she met a few people who tried to help her along the bumpy pathway after she nearly veered off into a tree or two. They were *chipper,* to say the least, much different from some New Yorkers' rude demeanor. Well, she did want a new experience, and this was it.

Once she finished exploring the bike trails, she went to the novelty shop to engage in retail therapy. There she found a guardian angel figure engraved with "*Never ski faster than your guardian angel can fly.*" She thought that was cute, so she purchased it along with a few other items then headed back to the lodge.

Coffee settled down before making dinner. She was happy O'Leary's assistant stocked the cabinets before she arrived. Although she had a running tab at the lodge's diner, she was trying a bit of a healthier lifestyle by transitioning to vegan; having hamburgers and fries wouldn't cut it. Tonight Coffee had a taste for Potatoes and Porcini Mushroom Ravioli in Broccoli Cream Sauce. Tomorrow she would make Somalian pasta without red meat but with Seitan and cauliflower.

Following dinner, Coffee wanted to do a bit of reading by the fireplace. She was reading a book, *Indiscretions* by Lotus R Flower, and it was just getting to the pinnacle of the plot.

"What a plot twist? I would have never thought of that!" Coffee said to herself.

Just as she closed the book to get some rest, her cell phone rang.

"Hello," she answered cheerily.

"Coffee, it's me, O'Leary. How do you like the arrangements?"

"They are wonderful. So much so I never want to return to city life."

"Glad to hear it. If all goes well, you'll have an assistant like mine."

"For real, Mr. O'Leary?" Coffee questioned. Never in her wildest dreams would she imagined that the deal she made with O'Leary would turn out to be so enticing. An assistant? Hell, her job was assisting others, not being the one assisted.

"I kid you not," he confirmed. "Anyway, I don't want to hold you. I only wanted to make sure the arrangements were to your liking. Oh, by the way, did you like the apple spice soap? I know it's your favorite."

"Yes, very much so but tell me….how did you know that?"

"It's my job to know. Understand one doesn't get to run a billion-dollar company by not knowing."

“Oh, you did your research?” Coffee said, not quite sure how to digest O’Leary’s answer. Finally, she decided not to make too much of the conversation. He was right. It is a high-paid executive’s job to know insider details others were not privy to.

Coffee let the matter drop. The pair said their goodbyes, and Coffee headed to the bathroom to shower once again. She lathered up but still felt a bit uneasy about O’Leary and the fragrance. After rinsing off, she dressed in her comfy red flannel nightgown then climbed into the bed. She slept peacefully, the best rest she had in years.

Chapter 3

When Coffee awoke in the morning, the peace she felt the night before was broken. She had several messages from a former client who threatened to defame her reputation if she didn't help him out of a certain catastrophe.

It was his own doing. Coffee managed her business affairs ethically. She would never do anything to jeopardize her reputation. As a result, she contacted her lawyer and best friendTiara. Tiara was a woman raised in the *hood,* but she wasn't the average hood chick. Tiara was a woman who, like Coffee, wanted more than the city life offered. Raised in and out of the foster care system since five, Tiara attacked her goals with enthusiasm. Tiara kept her head in the books and never let outside influences get in the way of her dreams.

Tiara maintained an A-average all through school and made the Dean's list numerous times during college. She passed the New

York State Bar exam on the first try. So, it was natural for Coffee and her to click. The only difference was although Tiara wasn't the average hood chick. She liked hood things, especially the men and twerking.

Upon contacting Tiara, Coffee informed her of Mr. Lawson's demands and how it was not a good idea to become involved in his business matters. Mr. Lawson was an ex-client for a reason, and Coffee wanted to keep it that way.

"Say no more, sis. I will send out a *'Cease and Desist* letter. I will inform Mr. Lawson that if he ever contacts you again, he will be facing harassment charges."

"Thanks, Tiara. I'm tired. I'm on vacation for a reason. To get away from assholes like Lawson. I just snagged one hell of a deal, and a matter like this could ruin everything I worked so hard for. Mr. Lawson is guilty of embezzling funds and sexually harassing his employees, even the males. I did not make him do it, nor did I give him the suggestion to do it. So, I don't feel as if I should be the one to clean it up for him."

"I totally agree Coffee. You don't have to worry. I will send the letter out and hold his balls to the fire should he contact you again."

"Thank you so much. You know I love you. Hey, I have a wonderful idea. I can speak to Mr. O'Leary to see if it would be okay for you to come to spend a weekend with me here at the cabin."

"In the woods, girl? No thanks."

"Why not? It's beautiful here. It's so serene. I'm sure you will love it away from the rats and rodents in the train stations and garbage piled on New York City streets."

"I'm not too sure about that. I'm a city girl. I used to hate visiting family in the south."

"You're older now. Circumstances have changed and look at it this way; it's only a weekend. It's not as if I am asking you to move here. You will love it, and if you don't, then when I return to New York, you get to pick our next excursion, and I promise not to complain."

"You promise?"

"I pinky swear."

"Cool, you better not renege either. Things like skiing are not on my bucket list, so I know when you get back to New York City, I'm going to have your ass in the hottest nightspot dropping it like it's hot."

"Tiara, you are a hot mess."

"I know but let me mind the business you pay me for. Be sure to send Mr. Lawson's email address in a formal letter to me via email to draw up this paperwork. He's going to be sorry he messed with you, sister."

"Thanks, Tiara. I knew I could count on you. I will have the fee transferred to your bank account within the next two hours. I see my so-called family also left a message.

Let me see what drama they have lying in wait for me, and I will get that information to you as soon as I check it out."

"No problem. Take your time but have the information to me by the end of closing tonight. I will work on the letter tonight from home and have it sent to him during business hours the next day."

"Thanks again. Let me grab some Chai tea. I need to prepare myself for the family dispute."

The two ladies laughed because Coffee's family was a bit dysfunctional, but the drama they caused gave even the corniest comedian the best material. After laughing about what could be wrong, the pair said their goodbyes, and Coffee got off the bed to stoke the fire, brush her teeth, and get dressed.

Coffee searched through her belongings. She chose a pair of black jeggings, a black turtleneck, and her brown construction Timbs. She wore the beige oversized North

Face coat to match the Timbs on her feet and a brown hat with the pom-pom on top. Coffee added gloss to her lips and a bit of black liner to her eyes. She felt on top of the world and hoped that the breakfast at the cabin's diner matched her mood.

XXX

The cabin's diner was everything she imagined and then some. It wasn't the average brick-and-mortar rest stop diner. Instead, the diner looked to be made of logs, very sturdy. The inside's atmosphere was astounding.

In the diner, there was an audacious fireplace which encompassed a roaring flame peeking through the black gate. The lanterns were placed strategically on tables, and the large circular wooden bar was made of glass with floral designs. The waitresses dressed in uniforms but not Mel's diner uniforms, from the television show Alice, type.

The waitresses had on all-black attire with smokey gray boots and fur placed around the top. They carried trays and moved around carefully, performing their tasks. The waitresses came in all shapes and sizes. I was surprised to see two sisters there. Of course, they were beautifully melanated and the messy buns perched on their heads with wisps of hair on each side made them look even more glamorous.

There was a lone male behind the bar. He had what one would call boyish good looks; blonde-hair swept to the side and piercing eyes. He was a bit on the slim side, but I guess it worked for him.

One waitress made her way to my table. I read her name tag, which stated Rachelle. 'Pretty name for a pretty girl,' I thought to myself.

"Hello, it's good to see you. Here's your menu," she said, giving me the signal that she was happy to see another black face in a sea of white faces.

I acknowledged her unspoken sentiment with the infamous 'black head-nod.'

I perused the menu when my eyes settled on a delicious bowl of oatmeal.

"It's good to see you as well. I know what I would like. I'd like to have the Cherry-Berry oats and porridge. A large bowl at that and the green tea infused with wild rose petals."

"Spectacular choice sista," Rachelle said winking at me. I winked back and we chuckled. She scribbled in her order pad then turned on her heels to place my order.

I stared around the diner taking in every sound and every movement. I noticed the patrons spoke in hushed tones. Being one from the city who was a member of 'Corporate America,' I had to wonder if it was my melanin they were speaking on.

Shaking off the vibes I was getting because I was determined not to let another person ruin my time here, I spotted the most gorgeous man. He was 6'3, brown-and-handsome. He had his hair in a tapered Caesar, and his goatee was razor sharp.

Our eyes connected. It was the most powerful. A smile immediately spread across my lips. Being so engrossed in my career, I rarely had time to date. However, I was on vacation and maybe; just maybe I could be willing to get to know someone other than the business men I have dealt with.

As we stared into each other's eyes, I wondered more about him. He was fine but what does he do for a living, does he have children, a wife, or even baby-mama drama?

Then I was jolted to reality, when Rachelle walked up and planted a kiss on his cheek.

"Oh," I whispered. "That must be her guy. So, I guess another one bites the dust."

Black love was beautiful, and I wanted to experience it. Not the struggle love but the true kind with minimal drama as I know all relationships hit a rough patch now and then.

“Rachelle, your order’s up,” The bartender yelled at her. She whispered something to the handsome man then went to the kitchen pick up area. Rachelle was carrying my order to me. Once she arrived I decided to do a little digging.

“So, is that your guy? You two make a wonderful couple.”

“Huh? Oh no, that’s my brother Desmond. He is here for a business meeting.”

“Oh okay, I thought,” I laughed it off.

“He’s single if you’re wondering,” she said, calling me out.

“Well, that’s good to know. I am too. Maybe I will see him around but please don’t say anything. If we connect, I would like for it to be organic.”

“I understand,”Rachelle assured me. “Listen, he’s a good dude in case you want the hook up and organic doesn't seem to happen swiftly."

Rachelle winked at me as she set my food before me. She gave me another smile.

"Well, let me go. I want to spend some time with my brother before his big meeting. This could literally provide generational wealth for the family. I am excited."

I watched as Rachelle excitedly bounced off to go speak with her brother. I wondered what type of meeting and who it was with? Yes, I am nosey that way but decided I might as well mind the business that pays me for I had bigger fish to fry by the name of Mr. Lawson.

I looked at my bowl of steaming porridge and I dug in. The chia and yogurt blended perfectly together and were delicious. After chewing a couple of bites, I took a swig of my tea.
"Ah, perfect," I thought to myself.

I finished up my breakfast then headed back to my quarters. I figured I would read until I fell asleep for a nap. Then a little later I'd either go to the gym or hit the bunny slopes. I'm a determined person and was dead set on becoming an advanced skier even if it killed me, literally.

XXX

Chapter 4

Around noon, I dressed for the slopes. Finally, I could get in tune with this lifestyle and afford yearly trips here. Hopefully, my newest client was the key to helping me achieve this dream. Until that came to fruition, I would enjoy the fruits of the gift bestowed upon me.

As I awkwardly attempted my best *hang n bang*, a technique the ski instructor taught us, newbies, to the slopes. It was a great feat after my sixth time trying when the chipper instructor said, “Okay, now onto our next technique, the *Christie Turn.”*

The instructor went into a fit of giggles with her last statement. Being the person I am, I had to ask her what was so funny. I wanted in on the joke.

"Oh, it's just that my name is Christie Turner. So, I find teaching a course that has the Christie Turn technique a bit amusing. It does something to my ego."

"Oh, okay," I said, cutting the conversation short. I was thinking the broad was ditzy. It was akin to me feeling the need to giggle every time someone said they wanted a black coffee, no sugar, no cream, which she mentioned. It just wasn't something I found hilarious as she obviously did. And I had to wonder how she even knew my name.

Deep in thought about the weird little encounter, wondering if I was making too much of it, I heard the richest baritone voice.

"Am I too late to join the festivities?"

"Why no, we still have a few techniques I want to show you guys," Christie said.

When I looked up, it was Desmond, draped in all his fineness. His striking demeanor did something to me, and his aura was even more powerful. I had to shake this shit off. I couldn't afford to become fascinated by this dynamic man; I just couldn't. There was something about Desmond that made me want to know more about him.

I caught myself wondering if he felt the same way until I noticed Christie was a bit too flirty with him. The sad part was he seemed responsive to her advances.

"Another color struck negro," I thought to myself. Simultaneously Desmond looked up and caught my glare. I shifted my stance from one leg to the other nervously.

"Hey, I remember you," he said, breaking the tension in the air I was feeling.

"I remember you too," I said, giving him my best smile while Christie stood by, obviously annoyed that Desmond's attention had been diverted elsewhere.

Desmond did the cool guy bop as he made his way to me. I saw Christie's face turn beet red, and I decided to stick it to her. I went in for the kill and gave my best Colgate smile. Desmond's face lit up. His whole swag was A1. We joined in pleasant conversation while trying to outdo each other practicing the technique shown to us.

"Alright, everyone. Now it's time to learn the parallel turn. Desmond, would you care to join me?" Christie said, trying to regain control over the situation, which was starting to feel like a tug-of-war.

To my delight, Desmond responded he was cool where he was, and he'd be partnering up with me.

"Well, we don't really need partners. I just wanted to use you as a prop for the demonstration."

"It's okay, maybe next technique."

Desmond turned to me and continued making small talk. I noticed the pause in Christie's demeanor and the glare in her eyes as she turned her sights toward me. I winked at her. I mean, she was cool and all, but we weren't friends, and for the hell of it, I'd show her what *Black Girl Magic* really meant if she continued to engage in this power of wits with me.

Desmond and I stayed on the slopes even after Christie's demonstration ended. We even became involved in a group snowball fight.

"*Boy, this trip is turning out better than I expected," I thought to myself.*

"Coffee, would you like to have some hot chocolate by the fireplace? I'd love to get to know more about you," Desmond inquired. "I promise I won't keep you up too late. I'll be the perfect gentleman and keep my hands to myself."

"I'm from New York, baby. So you better worry about those hands getting broken if you passed your place with me uninvited, that is," I informed him and gave him another Colgate smile and award-winning lustful stare in his deep eyes.

Desmond looped his arm through the hand on my hip, and we walked off the slopes smiling. I noticed Christie intensely staring at us. "*Shit, I don't know what her problem is, but she better watch out for my New York ass too. I come in peace, but if she doesn't remain peaceful, I'd have to hurt her ditzy ass,"* I thought to myself, not liking the vibes she was sending. *"She's probably just an entitled bitch, but she'd be entitled to an ass -whooping if she keeps playing with me."*

After that though, I gave Desmond my undivided attention. Why should I let the attention of such a fine-looking man go to waste worrying about a woman who didn't seem to be equal to one-third of me?

Xxx

Chapter 5

The next morning Coffee rises with the biggest and brightest smile. All she could think about was Desmond. They had hit it off so well. As she gazed out of the cabin window she pondered on what the day would bring. Coffee decided to get her day started. She debated about what she would wear in anticipation of bumping into Desmond. Her final decision was a long denim dress. The dress hugged her curves precisely before bellowing out after her hips. She paired this dress with her thigh-high red Christian Dior boots. Very happy with her choice of outfit, Coffee rushed to the shower.

After her long rejuvenating shower, she lotioned up her body. Coffee flat ironed her hair and applied natural-looking makeup. She accentuated with red lipstick making her ensemble complete also complimenting her chocolate-colored skin.

Coffee finished dressing and sprayed Gucci Guilty perfume on. She was a strong believer that certain fragrances attracted a pleasurable vibe and when she thought of Desmond nothing, but pleasure arose from the depths of her insides. Coffee grabbed her red Christian Dior purse and headed towards the resort's lounge. That's where everyone would meet up to socialize.

On the way to the lounge, Coffee would be so unlucky to bump into Christie. The two made eye contact and the tension coming from Christie was very evident. With that Coffee said, "Well hello Christie!". Christie tried being subtle, but Coffee peeped the way she stared her up and down before replying back "Hello". It was a very dry response, to say the least. None of Christie's antics bothered Coffee. As far as Coffee was concerned, a queen never steps off her throne to address foolishness. Coffee switched off to the lounge. She left Christie standing there as her red stilettos made a clicking sound down the path. Thank goodness there wasn't too much snow on the ground. She was trying to be cute for Desmond instead of safe for the environment. But 'oh well,' she thought, 'you only live once.'

Coffee entered the lounge. She was scanning the room while being very observant. She headed towards the bar area to order a Bloody Mary with the scattered hash brown platter. As she waited patiently at the bar her cell phone began to ring. The number was not blocked. Typically, Coffee would not have answers but due to the circumstances of this being a job related get away she answered.

"Hello, this is Coffee. How may I help you?"

The line was silent. Coffee says hello again and still no response. She hangs up and places her phone back in her Dior bag. She then began looking around the lounge. Coffee had a very unsettling feeling about that strange call. However, her stomach was louder than the thoughts in her head. She was starving and ready to eat. At that very moment, the waiter approached her with her order. Coffee pulled out her sanitizer, cleaned her hands, and said her grace. Now it was time to dig in but not before taking a sip of the Bloody Mary.

After Coffee finished her food, she headed towards the ladies' room to freshen up. As she headed down the long hall towards the ladies' room, she heard from a distance… "excuse me, do you need any assistance?"

Coffee instantly felt butterflies in her stomach. The male's voice sounded very familiar. She slowly turned around to look back; she was hoping it was who she thought it was. It definitely was. It was Desmond. He was standing at the other end of the hall looking so handsomely distinguished. At that moment, Coffee responded, "yes," without reservation.

The pair found a quiet spot near the lodge's window. Desmond ordered a spinach salad topped with vegan cheese and fresh fruits.

"A man after my own heart," Coffee admiringly stated.

“That’s nice to hear, but why do you say that?”

“A vegan man. There’s nothing like it. Plus, to see we have something in common is refreshing.”

“Well, you are what you eat,” Desmond responding tenderly.

“You can’t imagine the dates I’ve been on where I might order vegan lasagna, and a man is ordering a sloppy ¼ inch cheeseburger with bacon. The poor pigs, and I do mean the both of them. Then wash it down with a thick chocolate milkshake or diet cola as if the diet cola makes it all better.

Desmond and Coffee laughed almost to the point of hysteria when Coffee caught wind of an eerie breeze—then, turning her gaze outside of the window, she caught Christie glaring at the both of them.

“Geez, what’s her problem?” Coffee wondered out loud.

Desmond turned to the subject that captured Coffee's attention.

"She is a bit weird but probably harmless. Please don't let her antics spoil the moment."

"I won't," Coffee agreed.

The pair went back into having a light conversation. Desmond informed Coffee she looked ravishing in more ways than one.

Coffee was breathless, staring intensely into Desmond's eyes. There was a romantic pause and then a lean over the table for a sweet peck on the lips.

Coffee was delighted as the butterflies danced in her stomach. She couldn't remember the last time she felt like this when suddenly a bang and screech came from the window.

It was Christie looking every bit of Kathy Bates in her winning performance of Misery.

"My God. Let's get out of here," Desmond said, not shaken but upset that Christie could be so rude as to ruin his moment with Coffee. He signaled Rachelle so that he could pay the tab. Then took Coffee back to his lodge so they could recapture the vibe that was lost when Christie's madness started to show.

Coffee played it off as if she wasn't affected by Christie's outburst yet made a mental note to dig her mace and blade out of her luggage in case Christie did more than screech and turned beet-red. Coffee was lethal with a blade and wouldn't hesitate to give Christie what she was asking for if Christie tried her patience again. And that was on everything that Coffee loved.

Chapter 6

Coffee and Desmond spent time walking the grounds of the lodge until Coffee's feet started hurting.
'These damn boots!' Coffee thought to herself.
"Do you mind coming to my quarters? I really need to put on some hiking boots and a pair of sweatpants," Coffee inquired of Desmond.

"Sure, I was wondering if you were comfortable or not. I guess I got my answer."

The pair headed to Coffee's cabin when she almost slipped on a piece of ice. Desmond caught her and they stared in each other's eyes. It was such an intense moment that Desmond brushed his lips against hers and she responded favorably.
Much to their dismay there was a rustling in the bushes scaring them apart.

Coffee half expected it to be Christie's insane self but breathed a sigh of relief when a rabbit ran out on the trail instead.
Desmond continued with his kiss while gently stroking her hair. Coffee rubbed his back. Desmond softly picked her up by the legs and carried her the way to her cabin.
" What are you doing? Put me down I can walk."
"I'm not taking any chances in you falling and breaking one of your pretty bones."
Coffee giggled like a giddy school girl.
Desmond beamed with pride at his strength and the firm tone of Coffee's body.
He put Coffee down in front of the door. She used her key to open it while staring Desmond intently in his eyes.
They entered the cabin and he looked around. She kept a neat place. That was another plus in Coffee's favor.
Desmond grabbed her by the waist and pulled her close.
"You smell so good that I don't want to let you go."
"So don't," she breathed.
The couple danced to an inaudible tune only they could hear. Everything was going well,

and the vibes were great. Then there was a pounding on the door.

"Leave it. I'm not expecting anyone," Coffee stated not wanting their dance to end.

"It may be important," Desmond said trying to be the reasonable one.

"If it was important they would have called the room."

Coffee was making excuses as the knocking was persistent she could no longer ignore it if she wanted to.

She raced to the door with her heels clicking against the floor. She was livid. Coffee flung open the door only to find Christie on the other side of it with a weird look on her face.

"The front desk is trying to reach you. They say a Mr. Lawson has been calling the front desk asking for you. It's a bit frustrating for Jennifer who is new to answering the switchboard."

Christie gave half a smirk knowing that she interrupted an intimate moment between Desmond and Coffee. Hope wasn't lost in Christie eyes. There wasn't anyway that Desmond would pick Coffee over her. Christie honestly believed she could have

Desmond, but she needed more time with him to convince him. With Coffee around she didn't know how that would be possible. Sick of Christie's weird expression "Is there anything else?" Coffee asked her annoyed.
"Yes, May I speak privately with Desmond?"
Coffee looked Christie up and down knowing she had a few marbles missing. Coffee stepped back from the door then turned to Desmond who said firmly, "Not now. I will speak with you when I am finished spending time with Coffee."
Coffee was happy and closed the door in Christie's face who felt like kicking the door but screeched instead not wanting to lose her job. So she gained her composure and went back to the bunny slopes to teach her next class.
"The nerve of her," Coffee said disturbed by the interaction.
"Who is Mr. Lawson?"
"A former client who won't leave me alone."
Coffee told him the story and Desmond warned her to be careful. Between Christie and Mr. Lawson's antics and behavior

toward Coffee Desmond was starting to worry for Coffee's safety.

Chapter 7
Mr. Smitz

Desmond left Coffee's lodge on cloud nine. Coffee was not only beautiful but smart as well. He went to his sister's job to tell her about the luck he was having with Coffee when it seemed all hell had broken out during his absence. Upon further observation, he saw numerous employees crying and yellow police tape across the manager's office door.

Nervously Desmond looked around for his sister Rachelle. He spotted her and called her over to him to make sure she was alright.

"What happened here?"

"Oh goodness Desmond. I am so glad you are here."

"Calm down and tell me what's wrong?"

"Something bad happened to Mr. Smitz."

"Mr. Smitz?"

"The office manager."

"What happened to him?"

"I overheard someone say his throat was cut and a message in blood was smeared on the walls. Oh, God. Who would do something like this?"

"I'm not sure. There's no telling. It may be random, or it may be premeditated. Have to see what the police have to say."

No sooner than the words left Desmond's mouth did two homicide officers walk out of the office engaged in conversation.

"I spoke to most of the serving staff that was on duty?" a burly female homicide detective said.

"Yes, you did."

"Okay, I am finding it weird no one seemed to serve the deceased a lobster meal with a black cup of coffee on the side. There aren't any working cameras, and no one recalls seeing the deceased come in with a bag or have any food delivered. Plus the coffee was in a mug placed on a saucer with a rose beside it. Do you think we have a serial killer on our hands? Was the food items and placement a message Starks?"

"It very well could be Roselle," the golden-haired male responded.

"How do you want to proceed?"

"Let's allow CSI to fully process the scene then we can decide.

Rachelle and Desmond's mouths dropped open. They couldn't believe their ears. Was there a serial killer on the loose and if so who was the main target? Or could the killer's next victim work or live elsewhere? There were so many questions to be answered. However, when Desmond tried to get the burly detective's attention he was met with less than favorable results.

"Hold tight. We do need to speak with you. Just not right now."

Roselle the burly detective kept her stride to the hostess just rushing through the door. The hostess was Mr. Smitz's much younger wife, and it was imperative that Roselle and Starks didn't waste any time finding out if Mr. and Mrs. Smith we're having marital problems. Perhaps one was having an affair. If it were true and Mrs. Smith was the adulterer then she would be the detectives number one person of interest.

As the detectives talked to Mrs. Smith, Rachelle and Desmond engaged in frantic conversation. Desmond only worried about Rachelle's safety until Coffee entered. Then

Desmond's fear for one became fear for two as Coffee was starting to warm Desmond's heart.

Desmond couldn't help but notice Coffee's demeanor and relaxed look of Khaki Dickie cargo pants, North-face bubble jacket, and butter soft women Timberland boots change to one of panic. Coffee's eyes searched the room anxiously trying to take in the scene. Her face was becoming one of stone until she saw Desmond standing with Rachelle with whom she rushed to speak. They spoke in hushed tones as Desmond and Rachelle filled her in on the murderous event.

Coffee was horrified. Although she didn't know Mr. Smith this felt close to home as any one of the three of them could have

fallen victim to a predator's harm.

Desmond hugged Coffee reassuring her that

she would be safe.

Coffee then asked the most earliest question.

"Where was Christie at with all of this going

on?"

Chapter 8

Natural Disaster

With Mr. Smitz being murdered, Coffee called to arrange a flight so she could leave the lodge before time. A killer on the loose wasn't anything to take lightly.

Coffee called Mr. O'Leary to inform him of the current state of affairs.

"It's a shame that you won't be able to enjoy your full stay," he acknowledged gently.

"I know but with a dead body turning up and officers not having any solid leads it's best if I come back to New York City."

"How about you come back to New York, and we can find another, more suitable, and safe place for you to go on retreat? Maybe an island resort would be best?" Mr. O'Leary offered.

"That sounds wonderful, but I think I may skip the trips for now and just get to work."

"Whatever you decide is best for you is what will be done. I have a meeting now. So I am going to end this call, but you stay safe Coffee."

Mr. O'Leary hung up without waiting for a response.

"How rude!" Coffee thought. At least he could have given me a chance to say goodbye but then she had to take stock of herself. Mr. O'Leary had been more than kind and fair to her. Coffee regrouped by looking around her current space. How pretty and rustic it truly was.

However, Coffee couldn't wait to leave Vermont. For as pretty as it was, there was a dark cloud hanging over her. But as luck would have it an assortment of avalanches happened, one behind the other, where no one could enter or leave the resort.

So much for leaving early to go back to the big city, where ironically, Coffee would feel safer. Coffee was at a crossroads. Should she just stay in her room, or should she mingle more with the other tourists? Which one action would keep her from being harmed? Albeit there was strength in numbers, a killer may hide amongst the crowd and follow her back to her cabin. Only the Lord knows how she would survive such a scenario. There's no doubt that Coffee would defend herself vigorously, but the killer was armed. Then the thought occurred to her, "What if there were more than one killer?"

How would she have the strength to overpower and survive two assailants?

Coffee's mind was racing. Beads of sweat started to form on her brows. Coffee was working her way into a panic attack thinking of all the possibilities of being killed so far from home. "Who would bury me?" She thought.

"Or do I want to be cremated?"

Coffee did have a small life insurance policy but had to double check if it covered murder. The policy was something she invested into when she first entered the workforce. As a result, she didn't know too much about them. That would have to change and quickly. Knowledge was power.

Being from a big city such as New York, Coffee encountered numerous heart-dropping moments, but this murder seemed different. It was more methodical. For goodness sake what was with the cup of coffee and a rose being left at the scene of the crime?

Usually city crime was spree of the moment. One's anger getting the best of them but the Vermont killing was premeditated and the killer had a signature. This was something straight from the True Crime channels on cable.

Despite the fact, that Coffee felt nervous one advantage was she would get to spend more time with Desmond.

Unbeknownst to Coffee, Desmond had mutual feelings for her, and was hoping that despite the circumstances the situation with Coffee could become more serious.

The two also felt that maybe being snowed in the resort was a sign that things would work out fine between the two of them. This was sort of destiny and being stuck with each other was their fate.

Chapter 9

Killer Still Amongst Us

Coffee was deep in her thoughts when there was a knock at her cabin's door.

Apprehensively Coffee walked to the door. She had an iron stoker in her hand. If it was the killer he would be in for the fight of his life.

"Coffee, it's Desmond and Rachelle. Open the door."

"Desmond?" Coffee asked making sure she heard correctly. One could never be too sure.

"Yes, open the door. It's been another murder and we want to make sure you are alright."

Coffee hurriedly opened the door. After allowing Rachelle and Desmond entry Coffee looked out the door both ways to make sure that the siblings weren't followed.

Once realizing the coast was clear Coffee closed and locked the door. Desmond stoked the fire and Coffee shared her large hot chocolate with marshmallows into two separate cups for her guests.

"So tell me about this other murder? Is it related to Mr. Smitz's murder? Is the killer in custody?"

“Whoa, slow down Coffee. Let me answer the first question. Mrs. Smitz’s body was found about thirty minutes after she was questioned and released by the police and get this…”

“What?” Coffee asked while on the edge of her seat sipping her hot chocolate.

“There was a cup of black coffee and a single red rose left at the scene like with Mr. Smitz's murder,” Rachelle volunteered before Desmond could answer.

“So the murders are connected but is the killer finished their spree or will bodies continue to turn up?” Coffee replied.

“No one can tell us for sure. One thing’s for sure though…” Desmond began.

"What is that?" Coffee asked.

"With the avalanche and nobody allowed on the roads to travel the killer is still amongst us," Desmond finished.

"Damn," Coffee and Rachelle said in unison.

"I know but the good thing is that we three are all together."

"What's good about that?" Coffee asked trying to see Desmond's angle.

"There is strength in numbers. If it's one killer.."

"If!?" Rachelle asked frantically.

"Yes, use your head, Rachelle. There is a probability that there is more than one killer," Desmond said. "Now as I was saying if there is one killer he can't kill us all. We have the upper hand. He seems to kill his victims separately or he could have killed the Smitzs while they were together. Yet, he didn't. Why? I believe because it's only one of him."

"I believe that you are right," Coffee said and finished sipping the last of her hot chocolate.

Coffee looked over to Rachelle who seemed confused and at a loss for words.

"Rachelle?" Coffee asked trying to grab her attention.

"Yes , Coffee?"

"Are you alright?"

"As alright as I can be in this situation," she responded.

"I guess that is to be expected," Coffee said.

An awkward silence filled the cabin. Each occupant was not only worried about their safety but the safety of their companions. Each worried how they would survive being snowed in due to an avalanche with a killer on the loose. One thing was for certain, and two things were for sure, each was prepared to fight for their lives if need be.

"Coffee, may I use the restroom ?" Rachelle asked.

"Sure, let me show you where it is located.

Coffee walked Rachelle to the bathroom while Desmond placed a call. He abruptly hung up when Coffee reentered the room. “Everything alright?” she asked eyeing him suspiciously. Coffee wanted to know why Desmond hung up so quickly. Who was he speaking to and why he didn’t want her to know he was on the phone?

Coffee’s New York City instincts kicked in. The one’s that told her to never trust a person no matter how kind they may seem. Some people always had an ulterior motive. Now to figure out what was Desmond’s?

Chapter 10

Something Strange

Coffee kept glancing at Desmond. After the call he received something seemed off about him. Something was strange. Coffee couldn't quite put her finger on it but when he swooped in for a hug and kiss Coffee tensed up.

Desmond could tell she wasn't feeling his advances and decided maybe he overstayed his welcome.

By this time Rachelle had returned from the bathroom.

"Are you ready to go?" He asked Rachelle.

"Go? I thought there were strength in numbers?" Rachelle reminded Desmond.

"There is but I feel I have overstayed my welcome."

Desmond eyed Coffee trying to read her body language . Unfortunately he couldn't.

"No one has to separate," Coffee responded not truly feeling like being alone. Yet she was torn because how well did she really know Desmond and Rachelle?

"How about I go and get you ladies something to eat? With all that is going on I don't trust room service to operate in a timely manner."

"You may be right," Rachelle confirmed. "But maybe we should all go."

"I'll move faster without you two."

"Well, whatever we are going to do it should be soon. Before nightfall," Coffee inserted her two cents.

Desmond grabbed his coat, gave Coffee a big kiss, and Rachelle a hug. Everyone was awkwardly silent for a few seconds until Desmond came to his senses and raced through the door.

Coffee and Rachelle made small talk until they noticed it had been an hour and Desmond still hadn't returned.

There was a loud knock on the door.

"That's him," Rachelle said happily that her brother returned.

Coffee raced to the door and swung it open without looking through the peephole.

It was the detectives from the Smitzs' case.

"Yes, officer?" Coffee asked shocked to see them.

"May we come in?" Detective Roselle asked.

"Sure," Coffee replied then stepped to the side to allow them entry.

"And you are a waitress here?" Detective Roselle asked Rachelle.

"Yes and have been for the past five years."

"And Mr. Desmond Johnson is your brother?"

"Yes, where is he. He went to get us something to eat."

“Sorry to inform you but Mr. Johnson was found deceased twenty minutes ago.”

“Whaaat?” Rachelle and Coffee screamed simultaneously.

“As I was saying,” the detective continued coldly as her partner looked on stoically. “He was found deceased. Is there anyone that you two could think of that would want to harm him!?”

“No, my brother was loved by all who met him.”

“I have only known Desmond a short period of time. However, from what I could ascertain he was a cool guy. Not disrespectful at all. A perfect gentleman. May I ask how he died?” Coffee inquired.

"His neck appeared to be broken and he was thrown down the bunny slope. As with the other murders , a cup of coffee and single red rose was left near the body, but we need confirmation as to cause of death by the coroner," Detective Roselle's partner stated. Rachelle and Coffee was at a loss for words but then something came to Coffee's mind. Something she deemed important.

"Has anyone seen Christie the ski instructor?"

"Christie? Do you have a last name?"

"Perkins," Rachelle responded. "Christie Perkins. She's worked here for about two years."

"No, we don't know where she is. Any reason why you would mention her?"

"Well, she's weird. Plus, she had a thing for Desmond, but he was more interested in me."

"So you think she harmed Desmond and placed the coffee and rose in an attempt to be a copycat killer? To throw us off her trail?" Detective Roselle asked Coffee.

"With her, anything is possible."

Coffee explained the run-ins Desmond and she encountered with Christie while Detectives wrote down notes.

"This is all very interesting and should be investigated. Thank you for bringing this to our attention," Detective Roselle stated.

“No problem. We must get to the bottom of this so that once we aren't snowed in we could get back to some sense of normalcy. Also, Desmond deserves a proper homecoming service.”

“Oh lord,” Rachelle cried out in agony realizing her brother and best friend were gone. All she could wonder was why? Why her brother? What wrong could he have done in his life to become the victim of a sadistic serial killer? Which were also questions Coffee had as she silently prayed that anyone but her would be the killer’s next victim.

The detectives asked a few more questions and then left Coffee and Rachelle with business cards in case the pair thought of anything else that could help with the case. After the detectives left, Rachelle and Coffee hugged tightly and cried in each other's arms for the night. They awoke the next day red-eyed and hurting. Desmond's life was snubbed out and no one knew or understood why. Only the killer or killers would know. But hopefully, the detectives were worth their weight and could provide the answers everyone so desperately needed.

Chapter 11

Coffee tried to keep Rachelle as calm as possible. Rachelle and Desmond's parents were beyond inconsolable. They couldn't get into the resort to claim the body and with conditions, the way they were, no one had a timeframe on when their parents would be able to do so.

Rachelle went to the makeshift morgue to sit with Desmond's body. Coffee stood around in the waiting area as she didn't want to interrupt Rachelle's last moments with Desmond.

Coffee eyed the comers and goers suspiciously. Everyone was a suspect to her.

For the life of Coffee, she couldn't believe that she became caught up with a serial killer.

The landlines were down, and her cellphone only had two bars. She couldn't find where she placed her charger so she couldn't call her best friend during her wait. Coffee eavesdropped on a few conversations. One caught her attention.

"Hylton's body has just been found," a red-headed waitstaff told another.

"Hylton the tour guide?"

"Yes, the guide. Same m.o. Black coffee, red rose."

"Damn," Coffee uttered under her breath. "When will this end?"

"Excuse me?" the red-headed waitstaff asked.

"Nothing, I just overheard your conversation and I want to know when will the murders stop?"

"That remains to be seen," the green-eyed, fair-skinned staff member told Coffee. Her name tag read Sheryl and the red-headed name tag read Paula.

"Paula and Sheryl?" Detective Roselle asked.

"Yes," they said in unison.

"Detective Roselle. I have some questions to ask you."

"Sure," Paula said.

"Questions?" Sheryl asked a bit hesitant.

“Yes, questions. Is that a problem?”

“No, just wondering why ask me questions when you have a killer to catch?”

“Standard procedure to speak with a few of the people last seen with the victim,” Detective Roselle said sparking Coffee’s interest further.

Coffee tried to act as if she wasn’t listening, but the fact of the matter was she was engrossed in their conversation. Hylton had been so nice to her when she first arrived, it was hard to believe that someone would harm him. However, the same went for Desmond and they were both dead. Coffee wondered what on earth did the victims of the serial killer have in common? All victims were of various races and ethnicity, and none of their physical attributes were the same. It was as if the serial killer was drawing victims' names out of a hat. Coffee wanted to play sleuth and investigate the matter on her own, but she had limited knowledge about the situation. All she knew was that people were being found deceased and the killer left a signature rose and black coffee. That was hardly enough to go on if she wanted to play detective to crack the case.

Lost in her own thoughts Coffee almost missed when Paula said it was Christie who had been last seen with Hylton. Seemed the two had mutual interests in opening a truck stop and planned to have a meeting later on in the evening providing nothing happened. Yet, something did happen. Hylton was murdered and Christie was again nowhere to be found. Coffee was suspicious that every time someone has murdered, Christie was nowhere around. It was becoming routine.

"Coffee?" the detective asked drawing Coffee from her thoughts about Christie.

"Yes, Detective?"

"How are you holding up?"

"I just want to go home where it is safe."

"Hopefully we will have this matter wrapped up by the time the roads open and you'd be free to go."

"Good that is all I want."

"Us too," Paula and Sheryl chimed in.

By this time, Rachelle excited the makes it morgue. She looked a hot mess as the tears poured down her puffy eyes.

"I swear I will kill the person responsible for my sibling's death," Rachelle genuinely stated.

"I'm going to act as if I didn't hear that because I know you are upset but I warn you regardless of who was murdered I will run you in if you harm anybody," Detective Roselle stated.

Rachelle simply looked at Detective Roselle as if starting at a six-headed creature. She didn't care about jail. Rachelle simply wanted the person's head severed from their body and placed on a platter. Rachelle would gladly do life to make that happen.

Chapter 12

I'll Catch Up With You

Word was the roads wouldn't be cleared for another three days. Management tried to help attendees remain optimistic. They offered free continental breakfast and lunch for the three days for those who wanted it. Management also assured everyone was safe and to prove it they would hold a movie night equipped with a popcorn machine and fresh fountain sodas. Dinner wasn't a part of the package, but hors-d'oeuvres were which consisted of Quayle eggs on baguettes cut in small pieces with thinly sliced chorizo sausage wrapped in pancetta.

Complimentary champagne was also brought out on trays and carried throughout the main dining room for those who wanted it. The ambience was nice, and Coffee tried talking with Rachelle.

"Wow, I never had Quayle eggs before. Are they any good?"

"The best."

"Let me cut the small talk. How are you really holding up?"

"Can you believe they want me to go back to work?"

"Really?"

"Yes, talking about they are short staffed. I almost told them to fuck this job."

"I don't blame you. So are you going back to work?"

"This is me working. I am hosting. I am supposed to be working the room and will be when I feel up to it."

"You need to come back to New York with me and let me employ you. I'm sure even as a receptionist you will clear more there than you could ever here."

"Really? I make thirty thousand a year."

"Are you really stressing yourself for thirty thousand?"

"That's including tips," Rachelle said staring off into the distance. She never saw herself as a city girl but with Desmond gone and her parents retired in Florida what harm could it do. It would be more money, more opportunity, and more of a chance to find love she's been dreaming of.

"Rachelle, are you alright?" Coffee asked worries that Rachelle drifted off mid sentence .

"Yes, just thinking. How much did you say I could make?"

"I can employ you as my assistant and start you at fifty thousand per year. There aren't any tips, but the perks of traveling may be up your alley."

"I'll do it."

"Great, as soon as the roads clear we are out of here."

"I have to plan Desmond's homecoming services. It seems so cruel to have him on ice for so long. Mother nature has a mean sense of humor."

"Don't worry. That's just a shell of him. He has already transitioned."

"I hope you are right," Rachelle stated sadly. "Anyway, let me work the room. I'm going to need whatever money I can make for my trip to the Big Apple."

"More like the concrete jungle but you will get acclimated to city life in no time. I will help you."

"Thank you for everything," Rachelle said becoming misty-eyed.

"No need to thank me. We all need as helping hand at times," Coffee said genuinely.

"Well, I'll see you later, and Coffee…"

"Yes, Rachelle?"

"Did I say thank you?"

"You did. Get to work we can continue this talk another time."

Rachelle went off to work the room by greeting other guests. She was preoccupied when Christy walked in looking flustered. The detectives had questioned her for hours on end but didn't come to a reason to arrest her. Christie was almost at her wit's end. She locked eyes with Coffee and seemed to be making a beeline toward her when Christie was intercepted by Paula who had a million and one questions. Christie not wanting to be rude stood awkwardly as she feigned interest in what Paula was saying. Christie managed to mouth to Coffee

“I’ll catch up with you another time.”

This sent shivers down Coffee’s spine, but she didn’t show it outwardly but instead rolled her eyes and went to stick close to Rachelle remembering there is safety in numbers.

Chapter 13

Eavesdropping

Coffee followed closely behind Rachelle. Not wanting to worry her Coffee said everything was fine she was just a bit lonely.

"Well, it should be another hour or so and then I should be able to leave. Did you ever try the Quayle eggs?"

"I did."

"How were they?"

"Surprisingly good. I had seconds."

Rachelle laughed. Coffee made the funniest faces and was always animated when speaking.

Engrossed in their conversation, no one took notice that Christie was nearby. Christie was trying her best to eavesdrop but was failing miserably. Not caring what Coffee or Rachelle thought, Christie intruded upon their space.

"So ladies, who do you think the killer is? Oh and Rachelle, sorry about Desmond ."

"Thank you," Rachelle said rolling her eyes knowing Christie wasn't sorry at all. Christie probably was happy it was Desmond and not her.

Rachelle turned her back to Christie while Coffee kept an eagle eye on Christie. Something about Christie was off to Coffee. Coffee noted Christie showed her weird ways time and time again. Coffee thought on the time Christie screeched uncontrollably as Coffee had lunch and cocktails with Desmond.

'Could Christie have killed Desmond in a fit of a jealous rage?' Coffee thought to herself. Noting that Christie didn't have much to say but didn't leave the area Coffee speaks.

"Excuse me Christie but is there something we can help you with?"

"Just standing here in a public space. Is anything wrong with that?"

"Listen, I don't know or understand what you want from us," Coffee began. " But trust me, it isn't what you want."

"Don't speak to me in that manner or I might forget my manners and…"

"And?" Coffee said stepping in closer to Christie. Coffee was daring Christie to incriminate herself in all the murders that happened…especially Desmond's.

"And nothing. I have to go."

Christie takes one more look at Rachelle and offers her condolences.

"Save it," Coffee said having enough of Christie's insensitive demeanor. "She heard you the first time."

With that Christie walks away mumbling to herself. Christie was livid.

'How dare Coffee speak to me in such a way? I'll fix her," Christie thinks.

Coffee and Rachelle wait until Christie is out of their eyesight to talk again.

"What is her story?" Coffee asked.

"Christie? She is odd acting but harmless."

" I wouldn't be too sure. It's always the odd ones that commit murder. I know because I watch Dateline."

Coffee and Rachelle giggle at Coffee's dry sense of humor but Coffee's words tug at Rachelle's mind.

Rachelle always found Christie to be off but nothing to write home about."

Rachelle brushes off the weird sensation coursing through her and continues to make small talk with Coffee.

"Thirty minutes left until the end of my shift. Why don't you come to work the room with me?"

"Sure, I'd love to," Coffee happily responds. She was eager to take her mind off everything happening at the lodge.

The ladies worked the room. They greeted every guest. When asked questions about the murders Coffee tried to put their worried minds to rest by assuring them the worst had to be over. Some guests looked at Coffee relieved and others looked at her as if she was crazy. After all, there was still a killer on the loose. No one was in custody.

Coffee started to grow tired. She was in dire need of a good power nap. Coffee was almost ecstatic that Rachelle's shift was over.

The two ladies debated on whose cabin to sleep in.

Coffee wanted a change of scenery for the night, so they opted to stay in Rachelle's.

Rachelle's cabin was smaller than Coffee's and a bit more modern. Gone was the rustic atmosphere due to a large flat-screen television and surround sound radio system hanging on the wall. Rachelle had rose-scented Glade plugins. The room smelled like a florist shop. Coffee was at ease.

Rachelle made them both large mugs of hot chocolate with marshmallows and whipped cream. The mood was mellow, and they talked through the night about Rachelle relocating and transitioning to the city life. Coffee was ecstatic that she could help Rachelle during her time of bereavement. She knew in her heart that Rachelle and she would make it through the next few days unscathed but only if they stuck close together. And Coffee planned to do just that even if Rachelle grew tired of her.

Chapter 14

The Likely Suspect

One day and counting until the roads cleared. The detectives went door to door gathering contact information of staff and guests when a gruesome discovery was made.

Christie was deceased and the killer's signature cup of black coffee and red roses lay beside her corpse.

Rachelle and Coffee were shocked to say the least. Coffee was shocked more so because she felt Christie was the deranged person killing everyone.

Christie's murder just proved to Coffee that it wasn't always the likely suspect committing heinous acts.

"If it wasn't Christie then who could it be?" Coffee questioned Rachelle who seemed indifferent.

"I don't know but I told you Christie was harmless, didn't I?"

"You sure did but I am stumped now."

"Stumped?"

"Yes, Christie was always acting weird. To find out she isn't the killer is throwing me for a loop."

"Being weird doesn't make one a killer Coffee. Come on, you are smarter than that."

“Smart or not I have never been through anything like this. How am I supposed to know what to expect or what to think?”

“You’re right. Please forgive me. I didn’t mean to upset you.”

“I’m not upset. I just want to go home. I don’t want to be the next victim.”

“We made it this far and we will make it to the end. Please don’t worry. I got your back.”

“And I got yours.”

The two sat in silence for awhile. Then Coffee decided they should at least start packing their belongings.

“Why be here a second longer than we have to?” she asked Rachelle.

"So, true. We can head to your cabin and pack your things first. I should really wait for tomorrow because management still has me on schedule to work."

"Sure but let's do something. The quiet and non activity is getting to me. I don't want to be lost in my thoughts."

"I understand," Rachelle said as she was putting on her coat.

The two left out and headed towards Coffee's cabin. Immediately , the pair spotted a strange man dressed in a large Wool coat with fur, cargo pants, and brown hiking boots.

"Should we turn around?" Rachelle questioned.

"No, then he will know we saw him and exactly where we are. If we walk fast enough he won't be able to see the direction that we go in."

"Smart."

"Loop your arm in mine and walk fast," Coffee commanded.

Rachelle did as she was told, and they made it to Coffee's cabin in record time.

The ladies peeked out of the Cabin's windows. The out of place man was seen talking to Detective Roselle. Her partner and she slammed the man to the ground and slapped handcuffs on him.

Rachelle placed a call to her supervisor who wasn't aware of anyone being arrested.

"Give it sometime Rachelle. He just got arrested. Word on why will get out soon enough."

"You're right. I hope that is the killer so we can put these God-forsaken events behind us. Then there's still the matter of burying Desmond…" Rachelle said with her voice trailing off.

"I know. It will be alright Rachelle. Trust me please. I will be with you every step of the way."

"You promise? I mean you have already been so good to me. A job, a new chance at a better life. People I have known all my life had turned their back on me years ago."

"I'm not those people. I am Coffee Hart, and you will always have a friend in me."

Rachelle becoming mushy raced over to Coffee and threw her arms around her. The overpowering smell of roses wafted from Rachelle's clothing.

Coffee was taken aback because when did Rachelle handle roses.

Coffee chided herself for thinking such a thing. Rachelle lost her best friend amongst these murders. Her brother was her world. Anyone could see that.

"Coffee what's wrong?"

"Nothing. I am just ready to go home. You know back to a sense of normalcy."

“Nothing will ever be normal for me. My heart is gone.”

“I understand,” Coffee said feeling worse as Rachelle began to cry.

Coffee allowed her to weep without interruption. Then Rachelle received a phone call. She was needed back at work.

The girls headed out without a second thought of the out of place man. They were just eager to get the night over with so the could leave to a somewhat normal life.

Chapter 15

What the F*ck

The dining room was abuzz about Christie's murder. Some staff were inconsolable. It seems she made an impression on everyone whose path she crossed; whether good or bad.

Then for the guests to hear the man arrested was a transient with mental health issues it seemed a no-brainer to everyone that he was the killer.

Breathing a sigh of relief the guests let their guards down.

Soft music was playing, guests swayed back and forth while others ate watercress sandwiches. Some sipped champagne. All in all the emotions that ran high were now calming when a call came over the intercom.

"Ladies and gentlemen, the worst is behind us, and the roads have cleared. Everyone is free to start making plans to return home. As for us, we will be closing for renovations."

The guests gathered began to clap and cheer. However, for Coffee it all seemed too good to be true. Maybe it was because she was a city girl who was taught that if something seemed too good to be true then it usually is.

"What's wrong?" Rachelle came and asked Coffee upon seeing the troublesome look on her face.

"Nothing."

"Don't tell me it's nothing. Something definitely has you preoccupied."

"Just seems too good to be true."

"Excuse me?"

"Us, this, the roads clearing."

"All good things," Rachelle interrupted.

"So soon though? And I have been here for awhile, I have never seen that guy. All of a sudden he shows up and is the killer?"

"Yes, well he couldn't exactly announce himself. He had to keep a low profile."

"You're right," Coffee said not wanting to keep going back and forth with Rachelle about the topic at hand.

"I'm glad you see things my way. Now can you join in the festivities? How many people can say that they survived a serial killer spree?"

“I don’t know,” Coffee answered honestly and rose from her seat.

She and Rachelle went to the bar where Coffee ordered a Cosmopolitan. Rachelle went back to intermingling with the guests and all seemed well.

Coffee still had a nagging feeling that something wasn’t right with the scenario. However, she brushed her suspicions about everything to the side and enjoyed her drink. Coffee ordered two more before she began to feel woozy. Coffee had more than enough to drink. She informed Rachelle that she would be going back to her cabin to rest for awhile.

“Do you want me to walk you?” Rachelle questioned.

“No, I’ll be fine. The killer’s in custody, remember?”

“Yes, I remember smarty pants. Go ahead to your cabin. I’ll stop by after work to check on you.”

Coffee got up and left without responding. She was seeing double and wanted to just lay across her bed.

Coffee knocked out for the rest of the night. By morning Rachelle was banging on her door.

“The roads are cleared. The roads are cleared. Let’s go. We will take my car. I need to go to my apartment and make

Desmond's funeral arrangements. My parents decided he's been on ice long enough that the services should be held here. So they are flying in from Florida."

"Good, afterward we can head to New York City and get you settled into your new life."

The ladies loaded the gray compact sedan. Coffee was once again overwhelmed by the rose scent in Rachelle's clothes, now her car.

"What the fuck," Coffee said unintentionally out loud.

"What's wrong Coffee?"

"Boy, you love rose scents."

"Yes, rose scents are my favorite."

"I find that weird."

"You find everything weird. What else is new?"

"Nothing," Coffee said making mental note of the fresh rose bouquet that laid on Rachelle's backseat.

"Rachelle, where did you get the rose bouquet from?"

"Huh?"

"If you can huh, you can hear!"

"I don't have a bouquet of roses."

"Look in the backseat."

Rachelle looked and saw what Coffee was speaking about.

"I don't know how those got in here. Coffee, I swear."

Rachelle seemed just as perplexed as Coffee.

"Let's find the detectives. Who knows if the killer has a partner and you were the next victim," Coffee said concerned.

The two ladies made their way back to the lodge only to find out the detectives were transporting the killer back to the police station.

Not knowing what else to do the pair headed to the station to speak with Detective Roselle.

Detective Roselle was confident the right killer was in custody and that the roses left by the anonymous person was just a sick joke.

Rachelle and Coffee headed to Rachelle's house where they would bathe and talk about the rose occurrence. Rachelle's parents would be in town the next day, so the pair went to bed early. It was going to be an exhausting day, and both knew they needed rest and strength to get through it.

Chapter 16

Meeting the Parents

Rachelle's parents Desmond Sr. and Monica arrived as scheduled. Rachelle rushed into their arms. They all cried as Coffee stood off quietly to the side choking on her own tears.

"Take me to see Desmond. I want to see my child," Monica stated firmly.

"Ma, wait until he's transported to the funeral home. They assured me that his body would be picked up tomorrow at noon."

"That's a long time to wait," Desmond Sr. responded.

"I understand daddy, but his body isn't in the best condition. I don't want you both to live with those memories."

"You may be right," Monica sighed giving Rachelle a sense of relief. She never wanted to see that lodge again. It would be like looking back when her plans were to progress.

Rachelle introduced Coffee to her parents.

"My condolences," Coffee offered.

"Thank you. Rachelle tells us you were a dear friend to Desmond Jr," Desmond Sr. said trying to make small talk.

"Yes, Desmond was quite the gentleman," Coffee said.

"Wasn't any other way to raise him," Monica solemnly stated.

"Ma, daddy, would you all like a shot of brandy. You know to take the chill away from your bones?" Rachelle asked giving them a wink because that was always Desmond's excuse to sneak a bit of liquor when younger.

Rachelle and her parents laughed at the memory telling Coffee all about Desmond's antics as a young boy and adult. They told her about the time he stole his parents Mercedes to take a young lady on a date and got into a minor fender bender.

All in all it was a good evening with light drinking and a stroll down memory lane.

"Oh my goodness. It's getting late. Are you guys hungry at all?" Rachelle asked.

"Don't want to put you through any trouble," Coffee said.

"No trouble. There's a quaint diner down the block. They have the best buffalo wings and fries," Rachelle countered.

"Are there any vegan items on the menu?" Coffee asked.

"Yes, they just implemented the impossible burger to their menu."

"I'll take one without cheese, hold the mayo, just ketchup and pickles on the side."

"Got it. Ma? Daddy? Anything for you guys?"

"I'll take a real burger," Desmond Sr. said with a smile.

"I'll take a BLT," Monica stated, "Oh and heavy on the bacon."

"Sure, let me find the menu and place the call. Wait, what about something to drink?" Rachelle asked.

"I'll take a water with twist of lime," Monica said.

"Get me a good ole Dr. Pepper," Desmond Sr. replied.

"I'll take a lemonade," Coffee said.

"It all sounds great, but I guess I'll just take a black coffee," Rachelle said nonchalantly causing Coffee to become suspicious of Rachelle once again. All Coffee could think of was how could anyone who went through what they just experienced want a black coffee in life.

“Something wrong Coffee?” Rachelle asked before placing the order.

Coffee thought twice before responding that nothing was wrong, and she was just a bit tired.

When the food came Coffee ate in silence while Rachelle and her parents continued their stroll down memory lane.

After Coffee finished her food, she excused herself and went to shower.

She said her good nights then retired to the air mattress set up for her in Rachelle’s room. Coffee watched television until she dozed off. She never heard when Rachelle entered the bedroom and by the time she awoke Monica, Desmond Sr. and Rachelle were dressed and headed to the funeral home.

Coffee laid around in her gray pajama set and comfy slippers fighting the urge to snoop through Rachelle's belongings. Something about Rachelle wasn't sitting right with Coffee. Yet she couldn't exactly put her finger on it. One thing Coffee did know was that whatever happened in the dark always came to the light.

Needless to say, Coffee never did any snooping. She was happy she didn't after the trio came home. They were emotional about seeing Desmond Jr. in the funeral home. Monica was inconsolable to say the least. Desmond Sr. tried to remain strong for Rachelle and his wife but that was hard. Coffee chided herself for not having more trust in Rachelle. After all who would want to put themselves through such heartache. Coffee made a pot of tea and quietly left the family in the living room to mourn.

It was a sad day and Coffee tried her best to put her apprehensions to rest. She also tried her best to assist the family with anything they needed. By the time night came everyone was exhausted but managed to get some well needed rest.

In the morning, Coffee made scrambled eggs and toast for everyone. Desmond Sr. said Grace as Rachelle put on a fresh pot of coffee.

“Orange juice for me,” Coffee instructed.

“Are you sure?” Rachelle asked.

“Yes, very.”

They ate in silence then each went about their hygiene practices. Coffee was uneasy the whole day. If only she knew why. Hopefully, time would tell before Desmond’s funeral.

Chapter 17

Day Of

Desmond's homecoming service was beautiful if funerals could be considered as such. The funeral home decorated the viewing room in black and red which were Desmond's favorite colors. The family opted to dress his body in the same colors but instead of a tie, he had on a red bow tie. Friends and family traveled from near and far. His best friend Niles gave the best eulogy. Niles was dressed in all black and had tears flowing down his face. He was in agony and Coffee wished she could ease his pain. Yet she understood the devastation of it all. Desmond was a great guy. Coffee could tell from the moment she laid eyes on him. Desmond's parents had to be assisted by Rachelle after viewing his body. The blow to their hearts and soul were unimaginable.

After the viewing of the body and singing of the hymns Desmond's casket was closed and the body was taken to the gravesite to be his final resting place. The repass was held in a local hall and the food was catered by the diner Rachelle loved so much. She said it was one of Desmond's favorite places as well. The spread consisted of meat and vegan items. There were strong bean casseroles, macaroni salad, baked chicken,

Impossible sausages, and Impossible meatloaf with mashed potatoes and garlic sauce. The drinks were assorted, and attendees told stories of their fondest memories of Desmond. Some made Coffee become teary-eyed and some were downright hysterical that even Desmond's parents gave a chuckle.

After the repass Rachelle, Monica, and Desmond Sr. went home to sleep while Coffee stayed behind with the cleaning crew. It was a few hours before she made it back to Rachelle's place and she plopped on the air mattress still fully clothes where she dozed off until the wee hours of the morning.

When she awoke Monica was in the kitchen making everyone maple brown and sugar oatmeal. The house was smelling good, and Coffee realized she didn't eat too much of the catered food last night. Monica made her a hearty bowl and conversed as they are.

"So Rachelle tells me she will be going to New York City with you at the end of the week," Monica began.

"Yes, I am very much looking forward to it."

"Thank you. She is the only child I have left. Please take good care of her. I hear New York is a rough place."

"It is but I know how to maneuver through the mayhem."

“Oh goodness.”

“What is it? Did I say something wrong?”

“You said mayhem. My heart is heavy, and I couldn’t take it if something happened to my last living child. No parent should ever have to bury a child. Children are supposed to bury us.”

“I understand and am sorry for using such a disparaging word. I can assure you that Rachelle will be safe. Work, home, maybe an after-work drink but no real partying or going to dangerous places.”

“Whew, glad to hear that. Desmond Sr. and I always wanted to visit the big apple. This gives us more than enough reason to. Thank you, Coffee for being so kind during this harrowing time for us."

"Trust me, there are no thanks needed. I don't mind helping out where I am more than capable to do so."

"Well, I just want you to know you are appreciated."

"Thank you. That means a lot to me."

The two would eat the rest of their breakfast in silence.

Little did they know that holy hell was breaking out at the lodge. It seemed one of the maintenance men was found murdered. Left beside his body was a cup of black coffee and bouquet of fresh roses.

Chapter 18

When Coffee and Rachelle heard the news about the murder they were astonished. Surely the police had the right man in custody. But if so, how did the maintenance man get murdered? Police seemed to believe it may be a copycat killer. Even if so, the police had a job to do and that was put a killer behind bars.

The job was kind of tough because they had to find the guests from the previous murders and question then along with the resort's staff.

Coffee and Rachelle listened to Rachelle's parents rant and rave about their safety should the ladies decide to stay any longer in Vermont.

“The cops obviously have the wrong guy,” Desmond Sr. announced.

“What if he’s working off a list and you two names are on it?” Monica asked seriously.

“Mommy, we made it through the thick of things. If the killer wanted to murder us he could have done it already,” Rachelle tried to reason.

“I agree with Rachelle,” Coffee interjected. “We were on that resort for weeks. Nothing happened to us.”

“I still don’t feel right about leaving you girls behind,” Desmond Sr. replied to no avail.

Rachelle and Coffee's minds were set on leaving to New York City from Vermont in a couple of days.

The ladies accompanied Monica and Desmond Sr. to the airport. Each were lost in their own thoughts.

Once back at Rachelle's place an awkward silence filled the air. Coffee was the first to speak.

"Do you think we need to postpone going to New York City? I mean there's still an investigation going on?"

"I'm not postponing anything."

"We know that we didn't kill anyone."

"You sure are right about that."

"Good. So it's settled. Nothing will stop our going to New York City. City of lights and big action, here I come!" Rachelle exclaimed being overly dramatic causing Coffee to laugh.

"Girl, you are hilarious. On a more serious note, we should push our flights back. I have a feeling they want to talk with us, and I don't want to come back here once we are in New York. We will be busy."

"So, should we call them first?"

"I don't know. Why call first if we didn't do anything? Then again, we do want to get on with our lives. Let's think on it and make our decision by tomorrow," Coffee suggested.

"Let's take a walk. I could use the crisp air to help clear my mind."

"Yes, me too," Coffee agreed.

The ladies went for a walk and found themselves at a lovely boutique. The two bought a few items then grabbed a to go order from the local Asian restaurant. Rachelle ordered sushi and Coffee ordered noodles not wanting to eat any meat. They grabbed two waters and a few snacks from a grocery store then headed back to Rachelle's place satisfied with their purchases.

Shortly after arriving there was a knock on the door. It was Detective Roselle looking for a few answers as to which the ladies had none.

"Well, here's my card again ladies. Please give me a call should you remember seeing anything that could assist with solving this case. No matter how small you think the detail is it could be imperative to putting the killer in prison."

"We will," Coffee answered for the both of them then closed the door behind the detective.

"Guess what this means?" Rachelle said a little too giddy for Coffee's taste.

"I don't know. You tell me."

"That we are free to leave to New York."

"Right, no sitting around wondering if they will contact us because they already did."

" So we leave as planned."

"Yes, we leave as planned," Coffee confirmed.

Chapter 19

Coffee and Rachelle landed in New York City in the wee hours of the morning. The pair got on line for the yellow taxi car service for the next available car.

Once in the car Rachelle went on about how excited she was that Coffee would help her out. Coffee assured Rachelle that it wasn't any trouble at all.

"I have a fondness for you Rachelle. I only want to see you succeed in life."

"Thank you. I know a lot of people and very few have wanted to see me succeed."

“Well, you don’t have to trouble yourself with those people anymore. Let’s look to the brightness of our futures.”

“You’re right Coffee.”

The pair rode the rest of the way in silence. When they made it to Coffee’s place the two were exhausted. Both went to sleep fully clothed and without unpacking their luggage. Upon waking up Coffee realized that Rachelle was gone.

‘Now where could she have gone?’ Coffee thought out loud.

Coffee brushed her teeth, washed her face then placed a call to Rachelle’s cellphone.

Rachelle was walking back through the doors at the same time her phone started to ring.

"I'm here. I needed a walk to clear my mind and I bought us some food from the diner on the corner."

"You didn't have to do that. This is New York; every place delivers."

"I need to get to know the area. I can't expect you to allow me to be your shadow forever. Eventually I will get my own place and be on my own."

"I understand that. I'll try not to project my fears onto you. After all you are a grown woman."

"Thank you. Now let's eat."

The ladies continued to chit-chat about New York, the murders in Vermont, and Rachelle missing Desmond.

After eating they showered and headed for a day of sightseeing.

Rachelle really wanted to see The Apollo Theater in Harlem. There wasn't an event taking place, but Rachelle wanted to see it for historical purposes. After going to The Apollo Theater they caught a movie at Magic Johnson's Movie theater. It was a bit expensive for her taste but all in all it was a good experience. Since the ladies were in Harlem they decided to go to the soul food restaurant on Morning Side Avenue which was another staple in the Harlem area. It had been featured in numerous Hip-hop videos and the food was excellent. Coffee even broke her no meat rule for the occasion. She placed an order for their fried chicken, Mac and cheese, and collard greens. Rachelle had meatloaf which Coffee stole a few bites of.

"Goodness, I never thought I missed eating meat this much. I might have to incorporate a cheat day once a month."

"I don't blame you. Meat is so good," Rachelle said and the two laughed a bit. After finishing their meals the ladies placed a to go order so they wouldn't have to cook that night. Coffee reminded Rachelle they needed to go to the supermarket because eating out in New York City could amount to the price of rent.

The ladies decided they would go in the morning but for right now they wanted to go back to Coffee's house to relax.

They rode the subway back. That was an experience of a lifetime for Rachelle. She was in awe of the drummers who used buckets as drums, the singers with amazing vocal range, and the athletic abilities of the train dance performers who used subway car poles as their tool of choice. Then she became saddened at the homeless people with carts, some without limbs begging for change. Coffee watched Rachelle's every reaction as she dug deep in her pockets to give out spare change. Coffee felt Rachelle had to toughen up if she wanted to make it in the concrete jungle that everyone referred to as the big apple.

Once they made it back to the house the ladies freshened up and put on the television. A flashing news warning appeared. It seemed three people had been murdered. That was normal for Coffee to hear but what wasn't is what came next. Cups of black coffee and red roses were left near each of the bodies.

The ladies gasped and all Coffee could utter was "Dear God, when will this end?"

Chapter 20

Six months later

The murders ceased but the police didn't have any viable leads.

Coffee and Rachelle went about life as normally as possible.

Coffee assisted Rachelle in finding a small studio apartment in the area where Coffee resided. Rachelle was becoming acclimated to her new job and surroundings. Rachelle's parents visited twice. Although they liked New York City it wasn't a place they would relocate to.

Coffee was back to work as well. She had acquired some very high-profile clients. The contracts were lucrative, and she finally was able to save money. Real money.

Rachelle wasn't doing too bad in that department herself. She had opted not to get a traditional bedroom set but a futon. Rachelle didn't plan on entertaining company. Coffee would be the only one to visit her until she made friends. So she purchased a two-seat kitchenette dining set. She opted to paint her walls in pastel colors. With various artwork of mountains and hills decorating them. She also had a variety of pictures of her family and a large picture of Desmond near her kitchen area.

"Hello," Rachelle answered her ringing cellphone.

"Hey, it's Coffee. You have time to meet up today?"

"Sure."

"Good. I figured we'd go to Brunch then catch an afternoon movie."

"Sure. What's playing?"

"I don't know but I don't want to stay in the house today."

"I understand. Give me an hour to get dressed and I will meet you at the corner."

The ladies had a beautiful time, and all seemed right with the world. Each bought a take-out order of shrimp with broccoli from the local Chinese restaurant and then went their separate ways.

Coffee showered and put on her pajamas after eating. She called her best friend to catch her up with the details about work. Afterward she settled in bed for the night. Coffee had a peaceful sleep, and it was shaping up to be a good morning until she opened her front door only to see rose petals strewn about. Fear gripped her instantly. Coffee surveyed her surroundings then retreated into her apartment to find a weapon. Running into the kitchen she grabbed the largest knife she could find. Coffee quietly crept back outside and checked entrances and exit doors. No one could be seen. Coffee slipped the knife in her purse. She was on high alert as she made her way to the train station.

Coffee came up with a million and one reasons why rose petals should have been outside her door. None made any sense. It had to be the killer. Immediately Rachelle entered her mind. She reached for her cellphone to place a call to Rachelle. She didn't receive an answer. Nervously she turned around and raced to Rachelle's place. Soft music was playing and rose petals were on the floor. Coffee banged on the door. The music was turned up. Still no one opened the door. Coffee called Rachelle's phone once again disturbed by the events taking place.

She wondered if the killer had Rachelle hostage.

After a few more knocks and calls to Rachelle's phone she finally opened the door. Rachelle looked flustered as Coffee raced in.

"I've been trying to call you."

"Really? I didn't get a call."

"Listen, the killer is after us. We have to get in contact with Detective Roselle."

"How do you know the killer is after us?"

"There were rose petals in front of our doors. It could only mean one thing."

"That's true. Coffee have a seat so we can figure out what to do."

"How can you be so calm?" Coffee asked smelling the familiar rose scent.

"One minute. I need to show you this."

Rachelle disappears into the kitchen and comes back with a cup of black coffee. She set the cup on the table and then grabbed the bushel of flowers from off the kitchenette chair.

"Coffee, you are smart. I must give you that, but you aren't too smart, or you would have figured out that I am the killer."

Coffee gasped.

"So you killed your brother?"

"That was a copycat. You know people can't be original nowadays. Always stealing someone's ideas."

“My goodness. You’re insane. How do you expect getting away with murdering me in your apartment?”

“Easy. We went out for a date. You spent the night, and I ran an errand to the grocery store. Only to return and find your body.”

The look in Rachelle’s eyes was one Coffee never seen before. Instantly Coffee’s life flashed before her eyes. She said her prayers then reached for the knife in her purse when Rachelle turned her back.

Coffee plunged it into the back of Rachelle’s neck killing her instantly.

Coffee sat on the futon and cried her eyes out. She placed a call to the police and waited for assistance.

She didn't know how she would ever be able to rebuild her life, but one thing Coffee did know was that she would never go into the woods again.

www.ingramcontent.com/pod-product-compliance
Lightning Source LLC
Chambersburg PA
CBHW071248150726
48001CB00018B/408

* 9 7 9 8 3 5 5 4 7 3 3 3 4 *